The Lower East Side Tenement Reclamation Association

The Lower East Side Tenement Reclamation Association

David Rothman

OMNIDAWN PUBLISHING

OAKLAND, CALIFORNIA

2020

Cover art:
Photographs by David Rothman

Cover typeface: Viva Std, Interior typeface: Warnock Pro

Cover and interior design by Cassandra Smith

Library of Congress Cataloging-in-Publication Data

Names: Rothman, David, 1966- author.
Title: The Lower East Side Tenement Reclamation Association / David Rothman.
Description: Oakland, California : Omnidawn Publishing, 2020. | Summary:
 "Winner of the Omnidawn Fabulist Fiction Novelette Prize, selected by
 Meg Ellison. This magical realist tale follows the travails of a
 burnt-out Queens' teacher who spends his time obsessing over the fact
 that he has been cheated out of living in his Grandma Rose's Lower East
 Side apartment, and is thus priced out of his 'More Recent Ancestral
 Home', Manhattan, that is. Rothman weaves a rich story about real estate
 and memory. Daniel, our protagonist, is haunted by the remembrances of
 his childhood experiences in his grandmother's apartment. One day he
 discovers a hidden relic on Rivington Street, a tenement reclamation
 office run by an eccentric centurion named Hannah. When Daniel inquires
 about the chances of his reclaiming his grandmother's old tenement,
 Hannah is not impressed. "Things don't work like that, you rude, young
 schlub!" And so begins Daniel's journey to reclaim his past and to land
 an affordable space for his family in downtown Manhattan. This is a
 journey full of twists and turns, ups and downs, and an ending that
 would make even the most thick-skinned NYC real estate agent shake"
                                                      --Provided by publisher.

Identifiers: LCCN 2020023085 | ISBN 9781632430878 (trade paperback)
Subjects: LCSH: Memory--Fiction. | Real property--Fiction. | Tenement
 houses--New York (State)--New York--Fiction. | Lower East Side (New
 York, N.Y.)--Fiction. | Magic realism (Literature)
Classification: LCC PS3618.O86867 L69 2020 | DDC 813/.6--dc23
LC record available at https://lccn.loc.gov/2020023085

Published by Omnidawn Publishing, Oakland, California
www.omnidawn.com   (510) 237-5472
10 9 8 7 6 5 4 3 2 1
ISBN: 978-1-63243-087-8

For my mother, who laid books in my hands
on the shores of the Atlantic

Not a day goes by that I don't wake up and focus on the fact that I've been cheated out of my Grandma Rose's apartment and am now eternally priced out of living on the Lower East Side.

It's high noon on a rainy, autumn Friday and I smile as I pass a relic from another era, the fading Schapiro's wine ad painted on the side of a grungy, yellow building. There are some Hebrew letters on the bottle of kosher wine and, in trying to make sense of the ad, I remember a few Seders I attended as a child at Uncle Sam's on Delancey Street, all of us going through the motions, none of us believing much in God.

I walk back toward Felix's Tailor Shop at 91 Rivington and take an awning break at Steve Madden's boutique. I remember Grandma Rose's apartment being somewhere on the 100-block, but this can't be right because nothing on that street looks familiar. I scratch my head and try to conjure up the building's facade.

The last time I'd been inside the apartment was a few days before The Tragedy. I was playing a card game Uncle Sam had taught me called Casino on the front stoop with my sister Hester. I was seven that October afternoon, the autumn of Nixon's impeachment, and she, just three years older, dealt the cards so slowly, as if she felt the expanse of a whole lifetime in front of her.

'Moldavia House, 1891' is carved into the brown brick above the entryway of the next tenement, and I imagine the day when the bricklayer examined his just completed inscription, proud of his skilled work. I look around, soaking up the texture of the neighborhood's vibrant past. I dream of inhabiting the island of my Grandma Rose; of breaking bread in the flat where she tended to the psychic wounds of Aunt Ida, the only Kamenski sibling who made it out of Treblinka alive. I yearn to sleep again in the same bedroom corner where my sister Hester and I would stay up half the night making up Mad libs on Grandma's musty pullout sofa.

I step over a soaking A.M. New York in the gutter crossing on Essex, and call my mother with the distant hope that in an inexplicably lucid moment she may summon Grandma Rose's Lower East Side address from her patio lawn chair in South Florida.

I often ask myself how one can forget a meaningful address. How can one lose track of a specific location that played a central role in his childhood? It is hard to imagine a scenario in this age of GPS and Google Maps where high tech cannot rescue us from ourselves, where an app cannot save us from our amnesiac souls.

Mom's voice tenses up when she recalls anything about her own mother. "Daniel, who the hell knows the exact address? You think I remember? You've asked me this same question now a zillion times."

A bearded Hasid walks by with a white umbrella with some Hebrew words written across it. I can only make out a few of the letters. This realization is disappointing.

Mom continued: "It must be near the fabric shop. We used to walk a few blocks over to The Bowery to look at fabrics on sale. Piece of work, your grandmother. She hokt mir a chinick. Ask dad about your Grandma Rose and he loses his voice."

"Mom, Grandma Rose promised the apartment to me."

There was a hesitant pause on the line. I could hear my mother sighing.

"You were seven years old at the time. What kind of promise are we talking about?"

"Still, a promise is a promise."

"Grandma had completely lost it by then. The neighborhood was unsafe. There were pimps roaming the hallway of her tenement. Please!"

I open my eyes and notice the bearded Hasid, now half a block up, observing my movements. I turn and walk in the other direction, wishing I could call my mother now and hock her just a little bit more.

With most of the old businesses gone, replaced by Duane Reades and HSBC banks and with the overpriced creperie I just passed, I ask myself, why bother with this fool's quest? As my wife, Julie, likes to say, "Manhattan is kinda over."

What I'm trying to help her understand is that this 'obsession' of mine, as she likes to label it, has less to do with my need to live in a given borough than it has to do with finding my rightful place in a particular tenement on the Lower East Side.

The rain has slowed. I consider hopping on the F train back to Queens and relieving my sub of her fifth and sixth period classroom duties. Instead, I turn back toward Rivington, and have one of my therapeutic conversations with my long-buried grandmother on Essex. *"Grandma Rose, you could have given me the flat."*

"Speak up, Daniel, my shena punem. My ears are worn out."

"I said you could have set me up better with your apartment."

"I gave you the extra set of keys just after Aunt Ida jumped out the window. It was a few weeks before your mother forced me to move to the nursing home on Cherry Street."

I feel the jewelry box in the front right pocket of my black pants. I let Grandma's last thought pass. I'm feeling bad enough for playing hooky on my seventh-grade class.

"I have the keys. I just need the address."

I await her response, but hear nothing except an ambulance speeding down Delancey and a text alert beep from my Samsung.

"And Grandma, even if I were to find it, someone must be living there, and probably paying some insane amount."

I check Julie's text.

Honey, are u ok?

I buy a café au lait from the Moroccan café on Norfolk. The owner, a graceful elderly man from Tangiers smiles warmly at me as he stirs in the steamed milk. He probably assumes I live somewhere up the block. I'm becoming a regular.

I take a sip my as I work my way out to the sidewalk.

"Grandma Rose," I continue my conversation, *"I need your help."*

"You need my help? Life is hard. Be a mensch. I used to sell eggs on this street way, way back when I first came to this country. That's what we did."

"And how much rent did you pay for the flat?"

"The bastard had me paying $25 a month, can you believe it? Of course, that included access to the bathhouse around the corner."

"Any chance you can you tell me the address of the tenement?"

"Oh, Daniel, this much you must already know."

A few more gulps of coffee warm me up.

A Latina is shutting a third-floor window in the tenement on the other side of the street. Perhaps Grandma Rose's eggs had graced the kitchen table of this very apartment across the way some ninety years ago. Who can say it didn't happen?

I dispose of my coffee cup, lean against a tenement wall and pull the square Russian jewelry case out of my pocket. There are gold-plated Cyrillic letters stenciled onto the glossy wood. *Ювелирные.* With the care of a surgeon, I remove the cover and run my index finger over the two rusty silver keys sitting independently on a thin sheet of red felt.

ↃↃↃↃ ↃↃↃↃ ↃↃↃↃ ↃↃↃↃ ↃↃↃↃ ↃↃↃↃ ↃↃↃↃ

Julie slams the cupboard door. We are standing in our matchbox-sized kitchen making nasty faces at each other. We look like inmates, both wearing tacky red and yellow striped pajamas, bought a few summers back at a Bulgarian Black Sea Gypsy market. She squeezes my nose. "We can't go on like this. Promise me you'll see someone."

My wife, a dark-eyed Sephardic beauty, looks even sexier when she is infuriated. I turn away from her, toward the stovetop. "I'm making some chamomile. You want some?"

Julie opens the cupboard door and grabs a jar of honey.

"You've gotta stop with this key nonsense. You know, even if we somehow magically got into your grandmother's place, I'm not sure I'd even want to live there." She slams the honey down on the counter. "Screw the whole idea. Manhattan is for rich people, the 1%."

I try to take Julie's panicky tone in stride. She has been laid off from her therapist position at the hypnosis clinic for one month now.

I turn on the stove, and flip around to respond to Julie's outer-borough inferiority complex comment, and as I do, my left arm knocks the honey jar off the counter and onto the kitchen floor where it shatters to bits.

Julie yells, "Goddamit!"

I try to step back, but one of my socks is stuck in a gob of honey. Julie's already got the dust-buster out and is down on her knees trying to figure out if it will work on a glass and honey combo.

Clearly, the dust buster is making the floor situation worse. Julie takes out a couple of rags. She wets two and throws me one. We are both on the kitchen floor working hard to get back to the status quo. Julie looks over at me. "I think we should be talking about why you keep calling in sick."

I stand up and take off my soiled socks. Julie is still on the floor searching out any last pieces of glass. I say, "Babe, can you-"

"Can I what? CAN I WHAT?" Julie is waving her arms above her head like she's trying to kill a whole species of invisible bugs.

"Just calm it down a bit. Hester's not sleeping yet. She might hear us."

"I don't care whether she hears us or not," Julie says.

"We're fighting. People fight. Kids fight too. It's part of life. Why hide it?"

A few minutes later, we are in a calmer state, sitting on the couch eating pistachios. Julie says, "So, what's the point?"

"The point is that my grandmother sold eggs door to door, didn't finish high school and got to live on Rivington Street. Between us, we've got two Master's Degrees and we can't even come close to getting a place over there, in my ancestral home."

Julie covers her mouth, the way she does when she is just about to laugh at something I might take offense to.

"Your ancestral home is Pinsk or was it Minsk, not Rivington Street!"

I hold up my arms in protest. "Ok, my More Recent Ancestral Home."

Lying in bed, I am more than happy to flip over to my dark corner and call it another less than inspiring day, but Julie tickles my ears to get my attention.

I turn over and face her.

She says, "Think about it. Most of those immigrants living in the ghetto of the Lower East Side would've done anything to get out of the neighborhood. They would've been thrilled to live on a quiet, sunny street in Queens."

That's the last word I hear before drifting into an Oz-like reverie, a colorful journey of impenetrable symbols and delusional hopes.

Grandma, all fuzzy in early Technicolor, opens the jewelry box. The red felt rubs against her soft fingers, slow and soothing. "Have another rugelach, no? Her nightgown is stained. She cries out in frustration, squeezes my cheeks. Oy... poor Aunt Ida.

I journey over a peeling green fencing, jubilant. Then, it begins.

The keys are laid out on the table next to a 1914 edition of Der Forverts, a caricature of the former Mayor Seth Low with his ears swollen and half his front teeth missing graces its cover.

An unframed poster of the Arbeiter Teater Farband is torn on both of its lower edges, but manages to stay on the wall.

An ancient Eastern European woman with perfect nails is playing a waltz on a Steinway. She stops her fingers for a moment and says in an old-world accent, "You have the right to live in your ancestral home."

Three basement steps up and there is clothing; dresses, kerchiefs and stockings hanging in the claustrophobic space between buildings. A smell of smoked fish and fresh pumpernickel hangs in the air. A faded wooden sign over the entryway is only half-readable. 'The Lower East Side Ten.'

Back inside, she is singing, a mix of Yiddish and old Slavonic, such a sweet song for such a worn-out old woman. For a moment, she is young again, basking in her time. "You're a guest, no? You want some kishka. I just made some."

The next morning it is my job to get Hester to the bus stop on time. Julie has already rushed off to her Manhattan-bound train taking her to a mock interview.

I hear Hester, in the other room humming an Adele song. She has the habit of loitering in front of the bathroom mirror and playing with her bangs until the moment someone tells her that the bus is coming.

She strolls into the kitchen in about as much of a rush to leave as the Messiah is to come. She holds a butterfly hairpin in one hand and fills the other with the dozen or so chocolate-covered raisins that Julie has left out for her like a sugary mousetrap on the counter. Observing her now, I am reminded once again how much my daughter Hester resembles my sister Hester, not only in the inquisitive hazel stare of her eyes, but also in the way she likes to clasp and unclasp small objects in the palm of her hand. She shoves the handful of raisin treats in her mouth.

"Mommy says you're always complaining that you'd rather live in Manhattan."

"She told you that?" I feel the blood rising in the back of my neck. "Put on your shoes, we gotta move."

It's a beautiful October morning and we should be walking hand in hand, listening to the singing birds and enjoying a leisurely, father-daughter stroll. Instead, we are in panic mode, hustling like hungry pack dogs to catch a yellow school bus.

"Hurry up! We can't miss this next light."

"Daddy, is there something wrong with Queens?"

We scramble and just make the green, then turn sharply and quickly across the avenue.

"No, not at all. It's just," -and I'm thinking damage control here. "Manhattan has a bit more history."

"So what? Everywhere has history. That's what Ms. Kueffner taught us."

I pull Hester's hand forward and try to speed up a bit.

"Right, everywhere...has history, just not OUR history."

"Really, Dad?"

"There's an apartment in Manhattan that somehow slipped away from us." I run my hand through Hester's long black hair, then grab her arm tight. "There's the bus. We can make it." We run. "So, my grandmother, your great-grandmother, died way before you were born. Hurry! She used to sell eggs door to door in downtown Manhattan. Can you imagine?"

Hester ignores my comment and drags my arm toward the bus stop corner.

"Like really? You talk about the eggs' story all the time."

I give Hester a peck on the cheek. Before the bus pulls away, Hester opens her little window a bit and calls me closer with her index finger.

"Don't worry, dad, you'll find what you're looking for... Bye!"

We do the waving routine as the bus pulls Hester and the rest of the innocent children farther and farther away from what is left of any parental influence.

On the way to the car, I can't help thinking that I'd be a fool after such a vivid dream to not take advantage of another tour of the Lower East Side. I leave a message for Wendy, the school secretary on the way to the F.

⊠⊠⊠⊠ ⊠⊠⊠⊠ ⊠⊠⊠⊠ ⊠⊠⊠⊠ ⊠⊠⊠⊠ ⊠⊠⊠⊠

"So," says the Moroccan as he pours in my steamed milk, "You must live in the neighborhood."

I hand him a five and study how the milk froths around the periphery.

"Yes, of course, I live just up the street. Corner of Essex, or, forgive me, no, actually closer to Grand. Been there for years, but just discovered your wonderful place recently."

The old Moroccan laughs. "I'm glad you like my shop. It's good for business when locals discovering that I'm here."

He grins and hands me my café au lait, but I can tell by the slightly higher pitch in his voice that he doesn't quite buy my words.

A worker in a white smock rolls a cart of hanging pigs onto the freight elevator of the Essex Street Market. I watch the blood drip onto the pavement as the elevator door closes, and wonder what exactly I had said to make the old Moroccan suspicious of my neighborhood cred. I hear a text coming in. I check, assuming it's Julie. It's not. It's worse. It's Sharon, the assistant principal.

Good morning, Dan. Just wanted to inform you that you have now reached the allotted sick day limit for the school year. Do hope you feel better.

Two blocks south of the Moroccan, I notice something I haven't seen before. Just across from Felix's Tailor Shop at 97 Rivington, there's a peeling green wooden fence protecting what seems to be an empty lot. Strangely, I have passed this corner many times and have never seen the fence or the lot behind it. In New York City, the sight of an entirely new structure going up arouses mild interest, but this is different. This is a first time sighting of a structure that has clearly existed for many years. The logic doesn't add up. I look around, hoping to find solidarity with passers-by, but people rush by without noticing this phenomenon.

I dash across the street to examine a small red sign posted to the top of the fence. It's just an advertisement, 'Stop Bed Bugs' with the phone number of the service.

I peep through a tiny slat in the fence at a deserted lot of unkempt grass, the area closest to the sidewalk full of broken glass and assorted garbage. I am about to walk away, but when I take a second glance through the slat, I see a splintered sign at the base of the graffiti-splattered sidewall of 98 Rivington to my right, a dozen yards or so from where I am standing. The sign hangs lopsided over what looks like a basement entrance to the building, and reads, '*The Lower East Side Tenement Reclamation Association*.' My first thought is that I'm beginning to lose my mind. I check myself by looking away for a moment and then peeking through the slat again. The intriguing sign is still there, as real as the awning to Felix's Tailor shop across Rivington.

Instinctively, I hop over the fence, nearly ripping my pants on the uneven wood jutting up at the top. Standing in the grass, I can see the sign more clearly. I look away and then look back, but there it is.

I walk over to the sign and examine it, then look down the three basement steps and notice the light is on inside. I take a few back-steps back to the fence and look through the slats at the street scene on Rivington. A few taxis trickle by. Some tourists are checking out luxury, knock-off handbags laid out on the sidewalk. No one notices that a trespasser has hopped the fence.

Feeling dazed, I step over some Negro Modelo beer cans in the grass toward the basement entrance. Running my fingers over the faded words on the wooden sign, I mouth the word 'reclamation.' I stand in front of the entrance for a few minutes, contemplating whether I should take this absurd situation any further, or be prudent, call it an odd day and just go home. Could it be that there is someone working in the office down the basement steps that actually helps people reclaim tenement apartments? At the least, whoever is in there may have access to old neighborhood records, which might include my grandmother's address. I take the first step down toward the basement door, thinking it would be foolish to back out at this point. Curiosity gets the best of me. I give three soft knocks and then a couple pounds and it is then I hear someone undoing multiple locks before the door opens.

The woman who answers can't be more than four and a half feet tall and must be pushing a hundred. She pulls me in with her wrinkly hands. "Close the door behind you, for God's sake."

Her breath smells of fish. She shuffles me down an unlit hallway into a clustered office with a Singer sewing machine and an old Smith Corona manual typewriter next to it. There are stacked, coffee-stained copies of Der Forwart covering half the floor, and there, from right out of the dream is the caricature of Mayor Low and the unframed Arbeiter Teater Farband poster sloppily hung on the wall. She has the Benny Goodman Orchestra playing on a 33 rpm on an old player propped up on one of the newspaper stacks. She signals me to sit across from her rocking chair in a crude metal chair in front of the typewriter, then she plops herself down and begins to rock.

"Every twelve to fourteen years, some yuckel walks in off the street with a story." She holds up a brown winter sweater. "Meanwhile, I knit."

A collage of images from the dream parades through my mind. "You wouldn't happen to play the piano, would you?"

The ancient woman stops her knitting for a moment, and gives me an unpleasant look. "Do I look like I play piano? What do you think this is, some kind of variety show? I told you, young man, that I knit, that's what I do. Now, do you wanna talk business or should I get back to my knitting?"

I lean forward. "I'm sor- sorry. I just, just thought maybe-".

She continues to rock and knit. "The truth is I don't even wanna do this. I'm getting too old for all the tsuris. Manhattan ain't what it used to be." The old woman spits twice on one of the stacks of Yiddish newspapers. "I really can't do anything for you."

"But what is it that you do, I mean, when you actually do it?"

The old woman halts her rocking and scratches her mop of gray hair. "You look familiar. You sure you weren't just in here about nine, ten years back?"

"No. I was just out walking and happened to see the sign through the wooden fence. I was curious to find out what services you might offer."

The old woman lets out a low-toned chuckle and the sound of it jolts me a step backwards. "Services? Now we're talking about services. Oy gevalt! We stopped offering services before you were born."

I stand up, reaching in my pocket to make sure the two photos of Grandma Rose I've taken with me haven't fallen out. "But I thought maybe you, by the name on the-"

"Do me a favor. Don't think too much. You might break out in a rash. By the way, the name is Hannah, and the truth is, I'm getting fatigued by your presence. What kind of person doesn't have the decency to introduce himself?"

"Oh, I'm sorry. I'm Daniel." I put out my hand to shake hers, but she doesn't lift a finger. "I was hoping you might have some records of my grandmother's last apartment. Her name was Rose Horowitz."

I stare down at Hannah rocking away in her chair, clearly distracted, her eyes seemingly peeled to the Arbeiter Teater Farband poster just above her head, her arms crossed in combat position. It is then I hear the first irregular nasal inhale, the onset of a snore and realize that the old lady has fallen asleep. I throw my arms up in frustration and snap my fingers loudly an inch away from her left ear. Her eyes immediately pop open. "Ganef! Ganef! Thief! Don't touch the Singer. What do you want?"

"I'm not a thief. I just wanna know a little about how things work, nothing more."

Hannah yawns and offers me a disdainful smirk, makes an effort to stand up from her chair, and then falls deeper into it. She leans over and spits twice again on the soggy stack of fading Yiddish dailies.

"Things don't work, you rude young schlub." With her frail hands, Hannah signals me to leave. "They don't work anymore, and haven't for a good half century or so. Now, go back out the way you came in. And forget you ever seen this place."

I stand in place, wondering if any of this is really happening. A moment later, Hannah lets out a shrill shriek that has me dashing toward the door like the Road Runner.

ΣΙΣΙΣΙ ΣΙΣΙΣΙ ΣΙΣΙΣΙ ΣΙΣΙΣΙ ΣΙΣΙΣΙ ΣΙΣΙΣΙ ΣΙΣΙΣΙ

I can't sleep. I'm walking around at night in my red and yellow-striped pajamas mumbling nonsense about crumbling signs and nasty centenarians. Julie wants me to see a therapist. She slips on her matching pajamas. "Honey, what's disturbing you? It isn't that Lower East Side nonsense again?"

"No. Not at all." I slide into bed and turn my head toward the wall, hoping to pass a peaceful night without visions of Hannah haunting my dreams again.

In class, I daydream all day about obtaining grandma's apartment.

I turn my attention to the back of the room and Ronnie is practicing judo kicks against a world map.

"Sit the heck down, Ronnie, will you?" I bark out, as I hear my uncensored voice screaming in my head, *"Sit the f--- down, Ronnie or I'll break your little adolescent neck."* Never mind the potential Board of Ed. lawsuit, my war-weary eyes span a one-eighty around a classroom full of snickering punks loitering in every position imaginable except firmly seated at their desks. We have been reading *Of Mice and Men* for half the school year.

"Why did Lennie and George head for California?"

No one answers. Just more nasal snickering. I pace back and forth in front of the white board trying to recall the step-by-step of how exactly a younger and more idealistic version of myself had made the tragic decision to pursue a career as a middle-school teacher.

"What kind of work were they looking for?

No answer again.

I hear a familiar sound, a distant tapping and yes, Leticia has started a wave of text messaging again. I bend my head down and sure enough, most of the kids are toying with their keypads under their desks. Ronnie and his posse skip the cat and mouse charade, holding their cells out defiantly in plain sight, begging my rage. Enough is enough.

"I want all mobile phones on my desk right now, placed face down. This is an official weapons round-up." There are some predictable boos. Then the kids reluctantly lay down their arms.

I look around at this sampling of the class of 2020 and can't help thinking what a lovely century this 21st will be.

ꗞꗞꗞ ꗞꗞꗞ ꗞꗞꗞ ꗞꗞꗞ ꗞꗞꗞ ꗞꗞꗞ ꗞꗞꗞ

That night, with Hester already fast asleep, Julie paces around the kitchen with a cup of chamomile. "How were your classes today?"

I pour myself some tea. "Amazing. Truly inspiring. Every single student had their homework ready."

Julie smiles. Takes a small sip. "Did I tell you? I got a job offer during the mock interview."

I place my mug down and rush to hug her. "That's great news, honey. I'm guessing you're gonna take the job?"

Julie pushes my arms away and takes a step back. "Do you even listen any more when I'm speaking to you? It was a MOCK interview, so the offer was a MOCK job offer."

I sleep facing the wall again.

After the slight misstep with the Moroccan, I'm back, knocking at Hannah's door within forty-eight hours. This time, she seems to be expecting me, answering the door on the second knock. I follow her in through the tight space, nearly stepping on a Barry Sisters 33rpm lying sleeveless on the uneven hardwood floor. She plops herself into her rocker and knits for a few long moments before speaking.

"So young Daniel, do you keep a mezuzah on the side of your door, wherever it is you live?"

I give Hannah a quizzical look, my eyes gauging the direction she wants this conversation to go, and say, "Of course" to her question. She slowly inhales my suspect response.

"Well, that's important, Daniel. I remember your Baba Rosa saying something to me back in the day, on the night the lighter-haired Kennedy, the mensch, got shot. We were watching the California primary on the black and white," Hannah points at one of the office corners supposedly to point out the location of the TV, but there is no TV in the room.

"Rosa looked at me and said, 'We need to maintain our traditions to keep our head from going nuts, with all the fakakta blood being spilt in Vietnam,' and little did she know that the Kennedy boy's blood would be spilt just hours later."

There's an uncomfortable silence between us, and by the time the next words come out of my mouth, it's clear, in the way Hannah has suddenly stopped knitting that she has shared more information than planned.

"You knew my Grandma Rosa?

She shrugs and nods her head. Lowers her voice. "Yes, yes, Daniel, I did."

This is a lot to swallow. How could this hundred-year-old crab of a woman, hidden in this basement representing this fakakta tenement reclamation organization have any personal connection to my beloved Grandma Rose?

Hannah shoots a glance at the old phonograph still lodged on a second pile of fading Yiddish dailies. Benny Goodman's screechy clarinet solo plays through its shoddy speakers.

"Turn off the music, will ya?" Hannah covers her ears. "I can barely hear myself think these days."

I take the needle from the spinning record, my fingers still shaking from the revelation.

"She told me about the secret of the keys. I remember the Tuesday morning when your mother schlepped her to the home on Cherry Street. Your bubbe was a meshuganah by then, but she still had some of her marbles in place."

I stick a wad of gum in my mouth just to feel something moving. I say, "So you know she gave me the keys?"

"The one thing that remains crystal clear is your Bubbe telling me that she gave the keys to her precious granddaughter in an old Russian jewelry box."

"Yes, I was seven at the time." I make no mention of my sister.

Hannah stops knitting and smiles knowingly at me. I reach into my pants pocket and pull out the jewelry box. I open it to reveal the keys. Hannah gasps. "The Rivington flat!"

"What's the street number?" I ask.

"Couldn't tell you, but such a hamish apartment with five rooms!"

I take the keys out as Hannah bends forward in the rocking chair and swipes the box away. She runs her fingers over the red felt. "Now listen boychik, be a mensch. Forget about these keys. I'll have to do an investigation, research the old records, locate the current tenant and go from there."

She stops rocking for a second and makes a feeble lunge for the set of keys protected in the tight grip of my left hand. I've had these keys in my sole possession for nearly forty years. I'm not giving them up to someone I have known for some fifteen minutes.

Unflustered, Hannah continues in a business-like voice. "Don't get your hopes up about moving in anytime soon. We don't know yet who's inhabiting the place. My guess is that it is still rent-controlled, and would probably run you $700 a month, at least."

"$700!" I pronounce this sum like I am Lubavitcher celebrating God's name.

Hannah slowly pulls herself up from her rocker and limps two steps over to the table. She picks up a ballpoint pen and a dusty notepad. "I follow strict reclamation association rules. I'll do the investigation, even though I'm sick and aging, out of respect for your Bubbe. Now, there is a modest fee attached, which we can talk about later."

"Thank you."

"Zay gesunt. Now, let me take a long nap and if I'm lucky enough to wake up again, I'll get right to it."

I stand up, not sure how to conclude this awkward interchange. "Zay gesunt?"

Hannah frowns. "Zay gesunt. What, a Jewish kid and you don't know your Yiddish?"

I want to tell her that I once knew this expression as well as many other Yiddish expressions, but it's a world I've somehow forgotten.

"How pathetic are young Jews today. If you don't know the term, then look it up."

Hannah shoos me out with both of her hands, a now familiar gesture. "Go already, will ya, and don't forget to fill out the reclamation form with all your vital information on your way out. It's self-explanatory. Now, leave me in peace."

אאאא אאאא אאאא אאאא אאאא אאאא

I make sure the path is clear of cops and then hop back over the shoddy green fence onto a more bustling Rivington Street. I grab a knish at Yonah Schimmels to celebrate the welcome prospect of one day becoming a local and reclaiming a part of my family's history. Beyond my deep spiritual connection to the tenement, I can't help thinking, given our relatively tight budget, how much of a Godsend obtaining this rent-controlled apartment would be for us. With the savings, assuming Julie manages to get herself employed, I would no longer need to teach summer school, which would give me a blessed reprieve from the hell of spending more time with adolescent zombies than I do with my own family. I take a hearty bite of my potato knish and dream.

What I really need is a few days to digest it all; the mere existence of this association and the fact that there's a centenarian down those three steps that knew Grandma Rose. As I walk with Julie and Hester through the small monkeys' section of the Bronx Zoo on a cloudy Sunday, I begin to consider that these episodes haven't happened at all, and are just an extension of the dream I had a few nights earlier.

For three straight days I take the forty-six minute F train ride to The Lower East Side and walk by the Tenement Reclamation Association. Each time I'm tempted to greet Hannah, and to get an update on her investigation. But, on each occasion I decide it probably isn't wise to tempt fate, to risk upsetting the crabby investigator.

Julie is happy that I'm back at work and doing my job. Over a glass of Merlot, she kisses me softly on the lips. "I'm glad you are seeing a new therapist and have put this obsession behind you."

To get out of the doghouse with the school administration, I volunteer to serve on the perennially unpopular 'School Surroundings Clean Up Committee.' But I can't get my visits to the Tenement Reclamation Association out of my head. In class, I find myself day-dreaming about Hannah's musty, cramped office space.

The call comes Hannah-style, abrupt and matter-of-fact. I'm in third period at the end of my rope. I step out into the hallway, struggling to hear Hannah's feeble voice above the roar of adolescence ringing in my ear. "I did my investigation. Please come today at 12:30."

Luckily, it is a half-day and I don't have to feign yet another sudden virus. I'm over the fence and down the basement steps at 12:30 sharp.

Hannah answers the door with a half-smoked Kent in her thin fingers. I sit down in the primitive metal chair. Hannah falls into her rocker and begins to knit. "An elderly lady lives there—she's 107. I'm a spring chicken compared to her, I suppose." Hannah pauses. She looks up from her half-knit sweater and smiles. "She is paying next to nothing for the place."

My heart begins to race with images of piles and piles of disposable income. I straighten my back against the chair. "What does next to nothing mean, can I ask?"

"Next to nothing means around $650 a month, Yuckel. Isn't that about how much I told you it would be?" She points at the Singer. "Hand me that piece of paper on top of the machine over there."

I do.

"The address is 319 Norfolk, but, oy fuck!" and Hannah pauses, looking me sharply in the eyes like a wounded cobra. "It is a six-floor walk-up building with over a hundred flats and you will absolutely NOT be privy to certain items of information. Not yet, at least. One must be patient in such cases as this. We will simply wait for her to kick the bucket. I have offered her a nice gift to hand over the keys-"

I interject, gesturing to the pocket of my shorts. "I already have the keys. We just need-"

Hannah pulls herself up from the rocker and sticks her index finger in my face. She looks like she is ready to grab my chin and rip it off my face, but luckily doesn't have the energy.

"Don't even think of going over there! You would be breaking the Reclamation Association rules, and anyway," Hannah coughs three times, waits to catch her breath and plops herself back down in her chair. "Anyway, you have no clue which floor it is on and the landlord has most likely changed the lock in the last forty years. Don't invite tsuris into your life, young man. If you do, it will bite you back. You got it?"

The truth is, I don't get it. That is, I have no intention of taking Hannah's advice and sitting passively, waiting for an old soul living somewhere in the tenement at 319 Norfolk to die. With the grace of a repeat offender, I hop over the green fencing and jog the four short blocks to my grandmother's tenement.

I stand perplexed in front of 319, a somewhat rotted out brick tenement covered in bright spray-painted graffiti, with such favorites as 'I'll kill you again when you're dead' gracing the crumbling brick over the front doorway.

What confuses me is that I can't remember ever being here. Where is the stoop that I used to sit on? I don't remember the tenement being this far East, past Rivington, past Clinton, just a few blocks off the East River. Perhaps Hannah was playing with me, blurting out the random number, 319, as a decoy. I feel the Russian Jewelry box in my jeans' pocket and am tempted to take out the keys and try them in every lock. I ask myself, "What are five floors of keyholes when you've been waiting forty years to unlock a door?"

Yet, I hesitate. It is a busy time of the day, and surely someone will notice and report to the police that some demented, middle-aged man is sticking his key into everyone's door. Not the safest undertaking.

I need to think this through.

As we lie in bed with our matching pajamas, Julie runs her fingers over my ears. "Your ears are swollen. Something isn't right with you?"

I shrug off her comment. "What is that some kind of superstition?"

She examines the backside of my earlobe again. "Does the source of my knowledge matter? Your ears are telling me you're in some kind of trouble again."

Two days later, during our morning rush to the bus ritual, Hester says, "Mommy thinks you might be out of your mind."

⅗⅗⅗ ⅗⅗⅗ ⅗⅗⅗ ⅗⅗⅗ ⅗⅗⅗ ⅗⅗⅗

The Moroccan doesn't say a word to me as he pours in the steamed milk. I shrug off the nagging feeling that I should perhaps be in class. What is left to learn on the second to last day of the school year? He hands over the coffee. I cannot handle the silence. I speak. "Have you noticed how the bridge and tunnel crowd just take over this neighborhood on the weekends?"

"I notice many things." The old Moroccan takes my five and hands me back two ones. "I keep a close watch on what is going on around here." He gives me a warm smile, but the nature of his comment puts me on the defensive. I take a sip of coffee and feel the heat against my lips.

I start on the second floor because the one thing I can remember is my mother saying, "You wait down here while I go upstairs." Within an hour, I'm already trying my key on the fourth floor. The hallways smell like chicken soup and peeling plaster and are not well lit. Luckily, none of the tenants seem to be home at this hour as I snoop around the building. I pause as a guy with dreads hanging down from his helmet passes with his bike down the landing. I ignore a text from the assistant principal.

Something shocking and frightening happens when I get to apartment 5C. The key fits.

⋊⋉⋊⋉ ⋊⋉⋊⋉ ⋊⋉⋊⋉ ⋊⋉⋊⋉ ⋊⋉⋊⋉ ⋊⋉⋊⋉

She caresses my balding head with her feeble fingers. "Have some cookies. Have some milk, sweet Daniel."

I lay out the set of keys and the two photos on Sara's kitchen table.

"I remember this photo. It was taken in a studio on Hester, just across the street from a room your grandmother and I shared during the First War. The landlord was a dealer in smoked fish. The whole apartment smelled like Whitefish. Just awful."

Sara pours another half dozen Chips Ahoy cookies on my napkin. "Eat. You're under-weight. Where was I? The war ended. We both moved to different parts of Brooklyn, got married, had families and so forth. I lost touch with Rose, and then one day here's her brother Samuel at my door in Bay Ridge nudging me to move into her tenement back on the Lower East Side. He explains that his sister is moving to a home for nutcases, but she has never forgotten me and thought I might be more comfortable living back in the old neighborhood. I was an old widow. Who was I to say no to such a proposition?"

Sara wears a gray nightgown, a gray pallor of pockmarks and creases make up her face, a few thinning strands of gray rest on her head.

"Your Uncle Samuel tells me all about how his sister Ida, the only family survivor of the camps arrived penniless, and skinny as a stick of Wrigley spearmint. He explained how your sweet Grandma Rose, such a Zisseh neshomeh, took her in to her tenement flat, bathed her wounds every night, found Ida a job, and even left the flat to her in 1948 when Rose decided to move to a more spacious apartment in Brownsville to raise your already kindergarten-bound mother."

I dip another chocolate chip cookie into my glass of milk. I feel like a little boy again in Sara's warm presence. Her voice is calming and I am curious to fill in some more gaps in our family history.

"Samuel then tells me that Rose moved back to the Lower East Side flat after your mother got married. He explained that she never did feel at home in Brooklyn, and wanted to live out her golden years comforting her haunted sister Ida, who had never married, despite having had a suitor, a salty fish peddler, for a period of many years."

I throw the last of the cookies in my mouth, waiting for Sara to get to the part where Aunt Ida jumps out the tenement window. She never does.

Instead, she holds the second photograph to the light.

"We're all in our bathing suits at a studio on Coney Island Avenue. Rose is the one on the left, and I am the pretty girl right next to her."

With great care, she places the photo back down on the kitchen table. "If you're hungry, I heated up some chicken soup. I may look like an alta kaka, but I can still cook."

I tell her that I've just eaten. What I am hungry for is to get back to the topic of the keys. Sara rests her hand on my arm for a moment and reads my expression perfectly.

"Your Grandmother told me the story of how she gave the extra set of keys to her beautiful granddaughter. I've been waiting forty years for her to walk in. Is it Heather?"

I hesitate and clear my throat.

"Hester. It was Hester. But she died some months after Grandma Rose passed away. I've had possession of the keys for almost forty years."

Sara places her soothing hands over the nape of my neck. "Oh, you poor thing! You were at such a tender age and you lost your sister!"

I'm at a loss for words. Sara holds up a ladle. "Have some chicken soup. I won't take no for an answer."

The soup tastes like Grandma Rose's, thick and salty with soft pieces of shredded carrots and celery mixed into the chicken broth. As I eat, I take a closer look at the kitchen and small living room. There is evidence of fire burns on the kitchen walls, the hard wood floor is severely warped, most likely evidence of flooding, and there is a noticeable leak coming from the ceiling in the dead center of the living room. Sara notices my eyes roaming to all of the trouble spots, and shrugs. "I would have contacted the landlord a long time ago, but I didn't want to raise any suspicion given that your grandmother's name is still on the lease."

I try to change the subject by holding up the solo photograph of Grandma Rose. I say, "She must have been eighteen or nineteen in this photo. Was this before or after the period when she was selling eggs door to door in the neighborhood?"

Sara pulls herself up from her chair and puts her fragile gray hands on her hips. "My Daniel, your grandmother never sold eggs in her life, not that I know of anyway. Only the poorest of the poor did egg deliveries." Without asking, Sara took my bowl and refilled it with soup. "Rose was a talented seamstress with a respectable clientele. If she told you she sold eggs, this was probably after she had gone a bit cuckoo."

I shove a hot spoonful of chicken soup in my mouth. "My whole life, I've been told and retold the story about Grandma Rose and her eggs."

Sara grabs my arm, as if she has just remembered something she was supposed to have already told me. "An aggressive old bag came by a few days ago speaking some kind of gibberish about a contract and a valid reclamation of the lease. She came with a huge envelope full of cash, you know, a schmear."

I try to maintain an emotionless expression. "A schmear?"

"A schmear, a bribe, a schmear."

I want to ask Sara if she had, in fact, taken the cash envelope, but I don't want to risk upsetting the holder of the key.

"So Daniel," Sara places her soft palm over my bald spot like a yarmulke. "Your grandmother wanted to keep this apartment in the family and I want it to go to you when I die."

I almost choke on the wishbone.

"Of course, there is one condition, my boy. That until I disappear, that you check in on me every few days. Make sure this decrepit old lady hasn't fallen down and got her leg stuck in the radiator. I don't trust these home health people, they come and they go. I can't remember their names half the time."

"No," I say. "I can only agree if you promise to let me drive you out to Queens for a big dinner where you can meet my wife and daughter."

Sara smiles and seals the deal with as solid of a handshake a ninety-two year old woman can offer. "We do have one small problem we have to figure out."

My head begins to spin. "What's that?"

"My good for nothing son. Mordecai is waiting for me to die so he can illegally sublet the place for a handsome sum."

I stand up and pace around the small kitchen space. "You have a son? This is getting complicated."

Sara shakes her head. "Don't worry, Daniel. I want to give you the apartment. Rose would want it this way. We just have to find a way to cut my son out of the deal. As soon as Mordecai saw the chance to make big money, he left New York faster than the Dodgers left Brooklyn for Los Angeles. He never visits. All he thinks about is how to get rich like a Rockefella".

That night I compose the letter to Mordecai and mail it off to LA.

Dear Mr. Lipshitz,

It has come to our attention that your mother, Ms. Sara Lipshitz has been illegally subletting an apartment on 319 Norfolk for nearly half a century. While we do not intend to prosecute at this point, we would like to make it clear that our management agency will be issuing the lease to a new tenant within two weeks of the date Ms. Lipshitz leaves the apartment.

Sincerely,
Schapiro's Management

My only salvation during my two months of teaching hellish summer school is that every morning when I get up for work I am able to remind myself that this is probably the last time I'll do this for the rest of my life. I tell myself, once Sara passes on you'll be paying just $650 a month to live in Manhattan!

Hester learns how to roller blade in July. Julie and I celebrate our tenth wedding anniversary in August. Meanwhile, I check in religiously with Sara every couple days and while I tend to her needs, Hester comes to enjoy loitering outside the tenement with Julie the way I once had.

I come out the graffitied front entrance one Saturday afternoon and Hester is jumping rope on the sidewalk. "This plan of yours is truly insane," Julie whispers to me, beyond our daughter's ear. "I hope you know that."

ƆƆƆƆ ƆƆƆƆ ƆƆƆƆ ƆƆƆƆ ƆƆƆƆ ƆƆƆƆ

Sara leaves this life on a blustery cold Tuesday in late November. I'd be lying if I say that I do not grieve for her dear soul. Her son Mordecai, a real corporate smoothie, flies in to collect her belongings. On the day that he does, I'm there to greet him in my only business suit as a self-professed representative of Schapiro's Management.

"My condolences." I shake Mordecai's hand. "Listen, take an extra week or two to remove your mother's belongings if you'd like. That's the least we can do."

Mordecai sits at the same kitchen table where his mother and I had hatched up our devious scheme. "My wife and I were hoping to maybe move to the east coast and take over the place from her. It's too bad we can't work something out."

I smile at the lying bastard. "Well, clearly this was the case of an illegal sublet...but we don't have to go there."

"No, we don't."

On a blissful December day, Hester carries her *Hunger Games* backpack up the fifth floor walk-up and turns the silver key in the door of our Lower East Side apartment. She jumps up and down on the warped wooden floors and points at a framed photograph of another smiling girl named Hester hanging over the furnace. She waves at an artist standing at an easel in the apartment just across the street from ours. "I told you, daddy, you would find your golden ticket."

"That's right, precious." I pat her on the top of the head. Hours later, exhausted from moving in, lying in our new bedroom with a clear view of the Williamsburg Bridge from our window, Julie squeezes my cheeks.

"I still cannot believe you really pulled this off."

ƏƏƏ ƏƏƏ ƏƏƏ ƏƏƏ ƏƏƏ ƏƏƏ

Life is good, really, really good for a solid six months until Hannah knocks on the door one bright Saturday morning in May. She is exhausted from the walk-up, exhausted, angry and threatening.

Right away, without a word, I offer Hannah $4,000 to leave us in peace.

She says, "$4,000 a month, that is!"

"$4,000 a month? What are you nuts?" I look around to make sure this disturbance hasn't woken Julie and Hester.

"That's until I die. Keep in mind that I am ninety-nine years old."

"And what are you gonna do if I just say no and slam the door on your face?"

Hannah laughs, as if she has already anticipated the question. "Well, I suppose I'll just take a stroll over to Schapiro Realty and let them know there is an illegal tenant in apartment 5C. They can take it from there."

Hannah puts her angry hands on her hips, then sticks her pointer finger in my face. "I thought I made it perfectly clear that you should not interfere with the prior tenant. These were the Tenement Reclamation Association rules."

I want so badly to go ahead and slam the door on the witchy dwarf, but instead say "$3,000 a month, but not a dollar more."

I hear a shrieking voice coming from the Lower East side of my brain saying, "There goes your summer vacations." She puts out her bony hand and I'm tempted to break it before I come to my senses and shake it.

So this is a schmear!

Hannah hands me a white envelope with, 'The Lower East Side Tenement Reclamation Association' written in letterhead across its face. She smiles and waves good-bye.

"Enjoy our new and improved Manhattan. Remember, your first friendly offering is due by the end of the week. Zay gesunt!"

David Rothman has had short stories published in such journals as *Glimmer Train, Hybrido, The Piltdown Review, Newtown Literary*, among others. He has a Master's Degree in English and Linguistics from the University of Wisconsin, has taught writing at Queensboro Community College (CUNY) for over twelve years. He is the drummer for the New York City-based band, The Edukators, and is a proud resident of Jackson Heights, Queens (and has little or no interest in reclaiming his actual grandparents' tenement on the Lower East Side).

The Lower East Side Tenement Reclamation Association
by David Rothman

Cover art:
Photographs by David Rothman

Cover typeface: Viva Std
Interior typeface: Warnock Pro

Cover and interior design by Cassandra Smith

Printed in the United States
by Bookmobile, Minneapolis, Minnesota
On Finch 80# 340 ppi vanilla opaque vellum
Acid Free Archival Quality Recycled Paper

Publication of this book was made possible in part by gifts from
Katherine & John Gravendyk in honor of Hillary Gravendyk,
Francesca Bell, Mary Mackey, and The New Place Fund

Omnidawn Publishing
Oakland, California
Staff and Volunteers, Fall 2020

Rusty Morrison & Ken Keegan, senior editors & co-publishers
Kayla Ellenbecker, production editor & poetry editor
Gillian Olivia Blythe Hamel, senior editor & book designer
Trisha Peck, senior editor & book designer
Rob Hendricks, *Omniverse* editor, marketing editor & post-pub editor
Cassandra Smith, poetry editor & book designer
Sharon Zetter, poetry editor & book designer
Liza Flum, poetry editor
Matthew Bowie, poetry editor
Jason Bayani, poetry editor
Juliana Paslay, fiction editor
Gail Aronson, fiction editor
Izabella Santana, fiction editor & marketing assistant
Laura Joakimson, marketing assistant specializing in Instagram & Facebook
Ashley Pattison-Scott, executive assistant & *Omniverse* writer
Ariana Nevarez, marketing assistant & *Omniverse* writer
SD Sumner, copyeditor